00 400 994 764

KT-167-864

SIMON AND SCHUSTER

**SIMON AND SCHUSTER**
First published in Great Britain in 2012 by Simon and Schuster UK Ltd
1st Floor, 222 Gray's Inn Road, London WC1X 8HB
A CBS Company

Copyright © 2012 HIT (MTK) Limited. Mike The Knight™ and logo
and Be A Knight, Do It Right!™ are trademarks of HIT (MTK) Limited.
All rights reserved, including the right of reproduction reserved in whole or in part in any form.

Based on the television series Mike the Knight
© 2012 HIT (MTK) Limited/Nelvana Limited. A United Kingdom-Canada Co-production.

ISBN 978-0-85707-590-1
Printed and bound in China
10 9 8 7 6 5 4 3 2 1
www.simonandschuster.co.uk

© 2012 HIT Entertainment Limited.
HIT and the HIT logo are trademarks
of HIT Entertainment Limited.

# Mike THE KNIGHT

## and Trollee in Trouble

A knight is asked to do
many things—
search for monsters,
find lost rings!
There's one special thing
Mike wants to do—
be brave and bold in
a daring rescue!

There's one thing all knights must do – be bold and brave in daring rescues!

Mike and the dragons were playing in the Arena.

"I'm coming to get you!" called Mike. "You're not ticklish, are you? Tickle, tickle!"

Evie scooted past the Arena. "Do you want to play with us, Evie?" Mike asked.

"I can't stop. I have to get pepper and help rescue Trollee," Evie explained as she rushed off.

Mike was puzzled. "Rescue Trollee? But that's a knightly thing to do. Knights know all about rescuing."

"Perhaps they need magic pepper?" said Sparkie.

Mike had an idea.

**"By the King's crown, that's it!** I'm Mike the Knight and my mission is…to use my knightly skills to help rescue Trollee!"

Mike raced back to the castle and quickly got ready for action. He pulled out his enchanted sword and found…

"A feather? Oh well, I've got plenty of other knightly things to help me rescue Trollee."

Mike and the dragons collected all Mike's knightly equipment – his lance, trebuchet and his bow and arrow!

Mike and Galahad galloped to the rescue while Sparkie and Squirt struggled along behind them.

Trollee was stuck in a big tree.

"Trollee hungry?" Ma Troll asked.

"Some cupcakes would be nice," Trollee answered. Ma and Pa Troll went off to make some special cupcakes just as Mike and the dragons arrived.

"Don't worry, Trollee. I'm here!" shouted Mike.

"Great, did you bring pepper?" asked Trollee.

"You don't need magic pepper to rescue you. You need a knight! The best way to rescue you is…. pulling!"

"Squirt!" Mike commanded.
"Fly up and tie those short
vines together using a Knight's
Knightly Knot!"

Mike gave Squirt such
complicated instructions that
he ended up getting stuck!

"Great," Mike sighed. "Now I've got two rescues to do! Let's use the trebuchet. It'll be so knightly."

Sparkie helped Mike to set the trebuchet, but the spring went off early and launched Sparkie straight into the tree!

"Um…Mike. I think I'm stuck too!" wailed Sparkie.

Mike looked worried – "Err… no problem. I'll rescue all three of you. Somehow…"

"Mike," said Sparkie. "I think I feel a sneeze coming…ah…ah…"

"Oh no!" everyone yelled. When Sparkie sneezes he blows fire!

Mike ran over and held Sparkie's nose.

"Dat's bedder," Sparkie said, swapping his tail for Mike's hands.

"I know! I'll pull Trollee free myself," said Mike.
He swung on a hanging vine straight over
Trollee. He missed him completely and got his
foot stuck in a hole.

"Oh, no!" cried Trollee. "Where's Evie with the pepper?"

"But magic pepper won't help," said Mike.

"It's not magic. The pepper's just to help me sneeze. Whenever I get stuck, sneezing helps me wriggle out."

Suddenly Mike had an idea. He asked Squirt to flap his wings to make a huge dust cloud.

"Ah…ah….ah…CHOO!" Trollee sneezed and popped straight out of the tree, pulling Mike with him.

**"HUZZAH!"** called Mike just as Evie and the Trolls arrived.

"My Trollee free!" Ma Troll cried. "Thank you, Mike!"

"Don't thank me, Ma Troll," Mike said. "If I'd just waited for Evie, the pepper would have helped Trollee wriggle out. Now both my dragons are stuck and pepper makes Sparkie sneeze fire!"

"What makes Sparkie wriggle without sneezing?" Evie asked.

"That's it, Evie! **It's time to be a knight and do it right!**" Mike drew his enchanted sword and used the feather to tickle Sparkie.

"Oh no..please…don't!" Sparkie giggled as he wriggled around. POP! He was free.

"Your turn now, Squirt!" cried Mike.

"No! Stop!" Squirt squealed. "Oh, you have stopped…and now I'm free!"

"Next time you're stuck, Trollee, we'll have to tickle you!" Ma Troll said. "Cupcakes, anyone?"

"Getting tickled, getting trapped, getting rescued, getting cupcakes. My kind of day," said Sparkie.

Mike laughed as he tripped on a vine and landed back in the tree. "Woah! Oops! Can I be rescued, please?"

# HUZZAH!

# Mike the Knight

## More magical Mike the Knight books coming soon... HUZZAH!

Meet Mike!

Mike the Knight and the Scary Dragons — As seen on TV

Mike the Knight and the Mighty Shield — As seen on TV

Mike the Knight and the Fluttering Favour — As seen on TV

The King's Crown Sticker Book — As seen on TV — With Stickers Galore!

Mike the Knight: Mike's Missions — As seen on TV — Press the button. Be a knight, do it right!

Mike the Knight: How to Be a Knight — A POP-UP BOOK

**www.miketheknight.com**
www.simonandschuster.co.uk